Rosie THE RIVETER

Women in World War II

Sean Price

Chicago, Illinois

RAINTREE

TO ORDER:
☎ Phone Customer Service **888-454-2279**
💻 Visit **www.heinemannraintree.com** to browse our catalog and order online.

©2009 Raintree
a division of Pearson Education Limited
Chicago, Illinois

Editorial: Adam Miller
Design: Ryan Frieson, Kimberly R. Miracle, and Betsy Wernert
Photo Research: Tracy Cummins
Production: Victoria Fitzgerald

Originated by DOT Gradations Ltd.
Printed and bound by Leo Paper Group.

ISBN-13: 978-1-4109-3113-9 (hc)
ISBN-10: 1-4109-3113-7 (hc)
ISBN-13: 978-1-4109-3122-1 (pb)
ISBN-10: 1-4109-3122-6 (pb)

13 12 11 10 09
10 9 8 7 6 5 4 3 2 1

Library of Congress Cataloging-in-Publication Data
Price, Sean.
 Rosie the Riveter : women in World War II / Sean Price.
  p. cm. -- (American history through primary sources)
 Includes bibliographical references and index.
 ISBN 978-1-4109-3113-9 (hc) --
 ISBN 978-1-4109-3122-1 (pb)
 1. Women--Employment--United States--History--20th century--Juvenile literature. 2. World War, 1939-1945--Women--United States--Juvenile literature. 3. Women--Employment--United States--History--20th century--Sources--Juvenile literature. 4. World War, 1939-1945--Women--United States--Sources--Juvenile literature. I. Title. II. Title: Women in World War II. III. Title: Women in World War 2. IV. Title: Women in World War Two.
 HD6068.2.U6P75 2008
 940.53082'0973--dc22
                    2008011293

Acknowledgments
The author and publisher are grateful to the following for permission to reproduced copyright material: ©Associated Press **pp. 8, 24**; ©Corbis **pp. 11, 12, 13, 18, 22, 25, 26, 27** (Bettmann); ©Getty Images **pp. 5, 28**; ©Getty Images **pp. 19, 29** (Time & Life Pictures); ©The Granger Collection **p. 15**; ©Library of Congress Prints and Photographs Division **pp. 4, 7, 9, 14, 17, 20, 21**; ©National Archives at College Park **pp. 6, 16, 23**.

Cover image of a woman working on an airplane motor at North American Aviation, Inc., plant in California June 1942, used with permission of ©Library of Congress Prints and Photographs Division.

The publishers would like to thank Nancy Harris for her assistance in the preparation of this book.

Every effort has been made to contact copyright holders of any material reproduced in this book. Any omissions will be rectified in subsequent printings if notice is given to the publisher.

Contents

America Under Attack 4

Doing a Man's Job 6

Life on the Home Front 12

With the Armed Forces 16

Coming Home 26

Glossary 30

Want to Know More?............................. 31

Index 32

Some words are printed in bold, **like this**. You can find out what they mean on page 30. You can also look in the box at the bottom of the page where they first appear.

America Under Attack

December 7, 1941, was a Sunday. Most Americans were relaxing. But then they heard shocking news. Pearl Harbor had been bombed. Pearl Harbor is in Hawaii. Japanese airplanes bombed U.S. ships there. Many Americans were killed.

People learned about Pearl Harbor from radio. They learned about it from newspapers. They also heard about it from friends. There was no television yet. The news made people angry. They wanted to fight back.

Japan launched a surprise attack on the United States at Pearl Harbor. The raid destroyed many ships and airplanes.

After the attack, the United States entered World War II. The United States fought against the country of Japan in the war. It also fought against the countries of Germany and Italy. They were on the same side as Japan.

The war meant big changes for everyone. Men had to go overseas. They had to fight. Women had to do jobs men used to do at home. Women worked in factories. They drove trains. They grew food. They kept the country going. Women played a big role in fighting World War II.

5

Americans were shocked by news of Pearl Harbor. The attack forced the United States to enter World War II.

Doing a Man's Job

Before World War II, most women did not work outside the home. A woman was expected to be a wife and mother. Some women had jobs. They worked as nurses or teachers. But many people did not want to give jobs to women.

The war changed this. Many men had to go overseas. The United States **government** soon asked women to work. A government rules a country. One U.S. poster read, "Women—there's work to be done and a war to be won … NOW!" The poster showed women doing jobs that men usually did. They fixed cars. They made airplanes. They worked on big machines.

"**GOOD WORK, SISTER** WE NEVER FIGURED YOU COULD DO A MAN-SIZE JOB!"

AMERICA'S WOMEN HAVE MET THE TEST!

This poster shows the attitude many men had before the war. They did not believe that women could do hard work.

These women are hard at work building airplanes.

Women also served in the army and navy. Women served in all-female **units** (groups). These women did not fight. They did jobs away from the fighting. They moved supplies. They directed traffic. They drove trucks. The men who once did these jobs were free to fight.

unit group

Rosie the Riveter

Women worked in **factories**. Factories are businesses that make things. They helped the war effort. They built planes and ships. They also made guns and other weapons.

Many factory owners did not want to hire women. They said women could not use big machines. Some said women were not smart or tough enough. But factories needed workers. They soon rushed to hire women. "If you can drive a car you can run a machine," they said.

We Can Do It!

The United States needed women to build weapons and ships. Posters like this reminded women to make a strong effort.

WAR PRODUCTION CO-ORDINATING COMMITTEE

factory   business that makes things

Factory work paid well for women. Before the war, a woman might work as a waitress. She would have made $14 a week. During the war, that same woman could get a factory job. It paid $40 a week.

Women workers were given a nickname. It was "Rosie the Riveter." A **rivet** is a metal pin that holds things in place. Many women claimed to be the first Rosie. But the name really got started with a hit song called "Rosie the Riveter."

Women war workers were given nicknames. Two of the best known were "Rosie the Riveter" and "Wendy the Welder."

rivet metal pin that holds something in place

Eleanor Roosevelt

Eleanor Roosevelt was the wife of President Franklin Roosevelt. He was U.S. president through most of the war. He led the country.

President Roosevelt was in a wheelchair. He could not get around much. So Eleanor became his "eyes and ears." She visited many places. She visited soldiers who did the fighting. She visited sailors on ships. She also visited men who had been hurt in the fighting. Eleanor looked for problems. When she saw them, she told the president.

Eleanor also pushed to get women into the army and navy. She visited women working in factories. She tried to make life easier for working women. She wanted women to have better lives.

Throughout the war, she carried a prayer in her wallet. The prayer reminded her to work hard. It reminded her that men were fighting. They were dying for her freedom. At the end, the prayer asked "Am I worth dying for?"

This picture shows Eleanor Roosevelt pinning a medal on a hero of WWII.

Life on the Home Front

Women had to wait a lot in World War II. Men fought in far-away countries. They were sons, husbands, and fathers. A lot of them died. The areas where the fighting took place were called the **front lines**. People also did important work for the war in the United States. They called this work at home the **home front**.

This woman is placing a gold star in her window. She just found out that her son was killed in the war.

front line   where the fighting takes place

This woman lost all five of her sons in the war.

Women on the home front had to wait for news about the fighting. They did not know if their loved ones were safe. The United States let people know if someone was hurt or killed. The army or navy told people by sending a **telegram**. It is a brief message. A delivery man would bring the telegram to someone's house. People feared getting a telegram.

Families were proud of the men who went overseas. People hung stars in their windows. A blue star meant that someone served in the army or navy. A gold star meant that they had died in the war.

telegram　brief message

Rationing

Women at home faced many problems. They could not buy everything they wanted. Many items were **rationed**. That meant people could only buy those items in small amounts.

Metal had to be rationed because it was used to make weapons. That meant no new cars or bicycles could be made. People had to use old cars and bikes. Some types of food were rationed. Meat and milk were rationed. Clothes and shoes were rationed, too.

Women workers still had to shop and cook for their families. During the war they used ration coupons to buy things like meat and milk.

ration   sell in small amounts

Trains and ships were needed to deliver these items. But many trains and ships had been taken over by the army. Also, a lot of U.S. food and clothing was sent overseas. It was sent to help soldiers and sailors.

People could buy rationed items. But they needed ration **coupons**. A coupon is a small ticket. Each month, people got new coupons. People needed money and coupons to buy anything that was rationed.

This is what a ration book looked like. The coupons inside were torn out when a rationed item was bought. People were careful not to use all of their coupons early in the month!

coupon   small ticket

With the Armed Forces

Many women wanted to fight. But they were not allowed to. Most people still thought it was wrong to allow women in combat.

But the army and navy let women join. Women in the army were part of the **WAC**. That stood for Women's Army Corps. Women in the navy were part of the **WAVES**. That stood for Women Accepted for Volunteer Emergency Service.

Women in both groups stayed away from combat. They did jobs that freed up men to fight. Many did jobs that women had always done. They did things like typing and filing. But many women worked at jobs once held by men.

Women in the army and navy did jobs away from combat. Many were jobs that men had done before. This allowed the men to fight.

WAC Women's Army Corps
WAVES Women Accepted for Volunteer Emergency Service. It was part of the navy.

At first, many men made fun of women in the WAC and WAVES. But they soon stopped. Many women taught men skills they would need as soldiers. They taught men how to shoot guns. They taught them how to fly. After the war, the army continued using the WAC.

Are you a girl with a Star-Spangled heart?

JOIN THE WAC NOW!

THOUSANDS OF ARMY JOBS NEED FILLING!

Women's Army Corps United States Army

WAC and WAVES always needed more women. Posters like this asked young women to join and help out.

Nursing the wounded

Nurses in World War II were mostly women. Nursing work was hard and dangerous. Doctors treated men who were wounded in combat. Nurses helped the doctors. Many doctors and nurses worked near the fighting. They risked their lives to help people. Some nurses were wounded. Others died. Those who were wounded or killed received the Purple Heart. It was the medal given to Americans hurt or killed in the war.

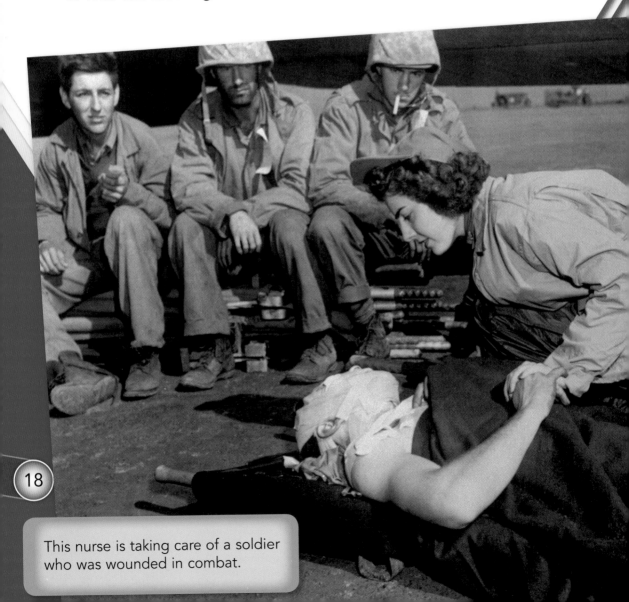

This nurse is taking care of a soldier who was wounded in combat.

LIFE

WANTED: 50,000 NURSES

JANUARY 5, 1942 **10** CENTS
YEARLY SUBSCRIPTION $4.50

REG. U. S. PAT. OFF.

This magazine cover says "Wanted: 50,000 Nurses." When the war started, many nurses were needed to help the wounded soldiers.

Newsreels and nurses

Television was not around yet during World War II. Most Americans watched **newsreels**. They were film clips shown before movies. Newsreels gave people news about the war. Many newsreels showed nurses doing girlish things. They put on makeup. They dressed in nice clothes. Those newsreels did not show that nurses risked their lives. They did not show nurses working in dirty, difficult jobs. Many Americans would have been angry if they had. They felt women should not do such work.

19

newsreel   film clips shown before movies. They told people about the war.

Covering the war

Many women worked as reporters. They went overseas and wrote about the war. They showed what life was like for soldiers and sailors fighting the war. They also wrote about **civilians**. Civilians are people who are not part of the army or navy.

Many reporters became famous. One of them was Thérèse Bonney. She was a photographer. Bonney took pictures of the war. Bonney looked closely at the problems of civilians. In World War II, many civilians were caught up in the fighting. Their homes were bombed. Their families were killed.

Thérèse Bonney's pictures showed people on the **home front** what the war was really like.

civilian   someone who is not in the army or navy

This cartoon shows some of Bonney's experiences during the war.

Bonney showed that civilians faced hunger. Most food went to soldiers. Also, many civilians had no place to live. They became sick living out in the rain and cold. Bonney risked her life to take pictures of these people. Her adventures were shown in a comic book. The comic book story was called "Photo-Fighter."

Spies

Some women worked as spies. Spies do things in secret. Many pretend to be for one side. But they secretly help the other side.

Josephine Baker was a spy. She was a black American. She was also a famous singer and dancer. Baker lived in the country of France before the war. Germany took over France in 1940. Baker stayed there. She secretly helped a group called the **Resistance**. The Resistance fought against the Germans. Baker hid information about the Germans in her sheet music. Her secrets helped defeat the Germans.

Josephine Baker was a very famous entertainer. She was also a spy! She risked her life to fight the Germans.

Another spy was Virginia Hall. She had lived in France. She showed U.S. spies how to behave like French people. She also went to France herself. Hall gathered news about the Germans. In 1944, the United States invaded France. Hall's work helped with the invasion. Hall lost a leg before the war. She used a wooden leg. The Germans knew she had a limp. But they still never found her.

Virginia Hall receives a medal for her brave work as a spy.

USO

The United Service Organization (USO) was a **volunteer** group. Volunteers do work for free to help others. In World War II, a lot of women worked as volunteers. People running the USO wanted to help soldiers. They wanted to lift the soldiers' spirits.

Soldiers often become **homesick**. They miss home a lot. USO volunteers made food for soldiers. They made sandwiches and coffee. They gave soldiers the food to eat while they traveled. Other volunteers sent books and magazines for soldiers. The USO also created special centers. Soldiers could go to these centers. They could relax and enjoy themselves.

The USO volunteer holding a bowl of cookies is Shirley Temple. She was a very famous actress.

The USO entertained troops while they were away from home.

The USO sent movie stars to visit with soldiers. The movie stars put on shows. One of the biggest movie stars was Bob Hope. He was a famous comedian. The soldiers loved these shows. Many USO shows were done close to the fighting. Many USO workers risked their lives to cheer up soldiers.

Coming Home

World War II changed life in the United States. During the war, women worked in many jobs. They could not have held those jobs before the war. They worked in factories. They worked in the army and navy.

After the war, many magazines said that women should stop working. Articles said that women should get married and have children. Many women liked that idea. They wanted to raise families. They did not want to work anymore.

After the war, families were very happy to be back together. But many women still wanted to keep their jobs.

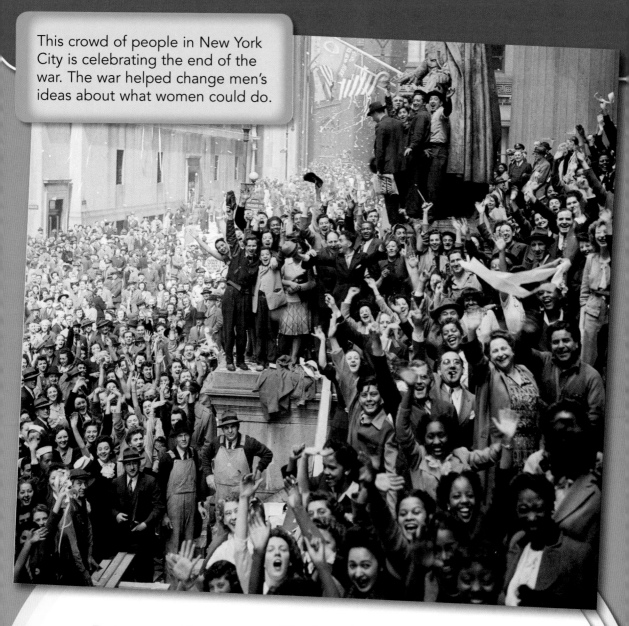

This crowd of people in New York City is celebrating the end of the war. The war helped change men's ideas about what women could do.

But many other women liked working. They made more money at their wartime jobs. They found it hard to give up those jobs. Working made them feel like they could take care of themselves.

The work women did during World War II changed attitudes. Women had shown that they could do almost everything just as well as men. Many men felt new respect for women. Also, more and more women chose to work outside the home.

Women hit a home run

During World War II, baseball was America's most popular sport. But baseball players were young men. Young men were needed to fight the war. So baseball teams lost their best players. Those players went into the army and navy.

People still wanted to watch baseball. So women became baseball players. The owner of the Chicago Cubs baseball team formed a league of women players. It was called the All-American Girls Professional Baseball League.

This picture shows the Rockford Peaches posing for a group photo in 1945.

Before the war, women were not seen as good athletes. Women's baseball helped change that view.

The teams had names like the Rockford Peaches and Fort Wayne Daisies. The players had to be good at baseball. They had to hit and catch well. But people also expected them to be young ladies. The players were sent to charm school. They learned how to look good and dress well.

The league was only supposed to last until the war ended in 1945. But many people liked the women's teams. The teams kept playing until 1954.

Glossary

civilian someone who is not in the army or navy

coupon small ticket

factory business that makes things

front line where the fighting took place

government group of people who run a country

home front life in the United States, where important work for the war took place

homesick miss home a lot

newsreel film clips shown before movies. They told people about the war.

ration sell in small amounts

Resistance secret group of people in France who fought against the Germans in WWII

rivet metal pin that holds something in place

telegram brief message

unit group

volunteer someone who works to help others for free

WAC Women's Army Corps

WAVES Women Accepted for Volunteer Emergency Service. It was part of the navy.

Want to Know More?

Books to read

Whitman, Sylvia. *Children of the World War II Home Front*. Minneapolis: Carolrhoda Books, 2000.

Williams, Brenda. *The Home Front*. Chicago: Heinemann, 2005.

Websites

http://www.rosietheriveter.org/links.htm

http://www.teacheroz.com/WWIIHomefront.htm

Both web addresses contain links to other websites about women on the home front in World War II.

Places to visit

Rosie the Riveter/World War II Home Front National Historic Park
1401 Marina Way South • Richmond, California 94804 • 510-232-5050
http://www.nps.gov/rori

Read *The Art of War: The Posters of World War II* to learn more about wartime America.

Read *The New Deal: Climbing Out of the Great Depression* to find out about how the Great Depression hurt many Americans. Learn how President Franklin D. Roosevelt helped get the country back on track.

Index

airplanes 4, 6, 8
All-American Girls Professional
    Baseball League 28–29
army 7, 10, 13, 16, 26, 28

Baker, Josephine, 22
baseball 28–29
Bonney, Thérèse 20–21

civilians 20–21
clothes 14, 15, 19
combat 16, 18
coupons 15

factories 5, 6, 8–9, 10, 26
food 5, 14, 15, 21, 24
France 22, 23
front lines 12

Germany 5, 22, 23

Hall, Virginia 23
home front 12–13, 14
Hope, Bob 25

Italy 5

Japan 4, 5
jobs 5, 6, 7, 8–9, 16, 26–27

magazines 24, 26
metal 9, 14

navy 7, 10, 13, 16, 26, 28
newsreels 19
nurses 18, 19

pay 9, 27
Pearl Harbor 4
"Photo-Fighter" comic book 21
photographers 20–21
posters 6
prayer 10
Purple Heart 18

rationing 14–15
reporters 20
Resistance 22
rivets 9
Roosevelt, Eleanor 10
Roosevelt, Franklin 10

ships 4, 8, 10, 15
shoes 14
songs 9
spies 22–23
stars 13

telegrams 13
trains 5, 15

United Service Organization (USO)
    24–25

waiting 12, 13
Women's Army Corps (WAC) 16, 17
Women Accepted for Volunteer
    Emergency Service (WAVES)
    16, 17
World War II 5